The

LIGHTHOUSE FAMILY

THE OTTER

Other books in the
Lighthouse Family series

The Storm

The Whale

The Eagle

The Turtle

The Octopus

THE OTTER

LIGHTHOUSE FAMILY

BY CYNTHIA RYLANT

ILLUSTRATED BY PRESTON McDANIELS

BEACH LANE BOOKS
New York   London   Toronto   Sydney   New Delhi

BEACH LANE BOOKS
An imprint of Simon & Schuster Children's Publishing Division
1230 Avenue of the Americas, New York, New York 10020
BEACH LANE BOOKS is a trademark of Simon & Schuster, Inc.
For information about special discounts for bulk purchases, please contact Simon &
Schuster Special Sales at 1-866-506-1949 or business@simonandschuster.com.
The Simon & Schuster Speakers Bureau can bring authors to your live event. For more
information or to book an event, contact the Simon & Schuster Speakers Bureau at
1-866-248-3049 or visit our website at www.simonspeakers.com.
The text for this book was set in Centaur.
The illustrations for this book were rendered in graphite.
Manufactured in the United States of America / 0216 PCH
First Edition
2 4 6 8 10 9 7 5 3 1
Library of Congress Cataloging-in-Publication Data
Names: Rylant, Cynthia.
Title: The otter / by Cynthia Rylant ; illustrated by Preston McDaniels.
Other titles: Otter
Description: First edition. | New York : Beach Lane Books, [2016] | Series:
The lighthouse family ; #6 | Summary: A family of animals that lives in a
lighthouse helps an otter, whose sister is trapped in an old fishing net.
Identifiers: LCCN 2015022829 | ISBN 9781481460453 (hardback)
ISBN 9781481460248 (e-book)
Subjects: | CYAC: Animals—Fiction. | Otters—Fiction. | Wildlife rescue—Fiction.
| Seashore—Fiction. | Lighthouses—Fiction. | BISAC: JUVENILE FICTION /
Animals / Mice, Hamsters, Guinea Pigs, etc.. | JUVENILE FICTION / Family /
General (see also headings under Social Issues). | JUVENILE FICTION /
Action & Adventure / General.
Classification: LCC PZ7.R982 Ot 2016 | DDC [Fic]—dc23
LC record available at http://lccn.loc.gov/2015022829

For Nugget
—*P. McD.*

Contents

1. *Help!* 10

2. *Dottie and Dooley* 18

3. *Dolphins!* 24

4. *Egg Island* 30

5. *Friends and Dumplings* . . . 38

1. Help!

On a tall cliff rising far above the sea stood a beautiful lighthouse, and in this lighthouse lived a happy family. But this was not an ordinary family. It was a family created by adventure, rescue, and love.

Pandora the cat had lived there alone for many years, devoted to the keeping of the light, and sometimes she had wondered if she might always be alone.

Then one day a storm had blown in a surprise: a sailor named Seabold and his shipwrecked little boat. Pandora helped Seabold mend, and he, in turn, mended his boat to prepare for sailing again. Seabold belonged to the sea.

But before Pandora and Seabold could say their good-byes, another surprise arrived: Whistler, Lila, and baby Tiny, three orphaned children who had been set adrift in a crate at sea. Seabold rescued them, and he brought them to Pandora for that which she gave best—comfort and love.

After this, still another surprise: Seabold gave up his sailing life. He decided to stay on at the lighthouse, to help Pandora raise the three small children. He felt they all might need him.

That is how the lighthouse family came to be.

It was now summer at the lighthouse, and chores were much easier, for there was no fog to threaten the sailing ships and no gales to blow the ships off course.

The lighthouse family could relax and play.

Of course, Whistler and Lila played all the time, summer or winter, but summer play was simpler.

They climbed over the cliffs, collecting wild onion for Pandora's summer salads. They sat quietly in the estuary and watched the Swans—long married—glide gracefully together. They laughed with the laughing gulls when the birds flew above their heads.

Baby Tiny stayed safe and warm with Pandora or Seabold while her brother and sister were out exploring. Pandora enjoyed tending her foxgloves or baking rose-petal muffins while Tiny slept deep in her apron pocket. And Seabold often carried Tiny in the roll of his cap as he made himself useful repairing the rock walls around Pandora's pea patch or building wooden sea horses for the children to ride.

"The children will love those," Pandora said

with approval as Seabold showed her one of the sea horses he had made.

"Tiny isn't quite ready to ride a sea horse," said Seabold. "So I made her a puffer-fish ball."

Tiny rolled the little ball across the cottage porch.

"Lovely," said Pandora.

This summer day was passing so peacefully that it was really quite jarring to everyone when suddenly the loud bell of a fog buoy out in the sea began frantically to ring. In fact, it was so alarming that Tiny scrambled into Pandora's apron and covered her tiny ears.

Whistler and Lila came running into the house.

"Otter! Otter!" they both cried.

"What do you mean, children?" asked Pandora as Seabold reached for his walking stick.

"An otter is ringing the buoy bell," said Lila, her eyes wide. "And he is calling for help!"

Indeed, an otter did need help.

And he had surely come to the right place to find it.

2. Dottie and Dooley

With Pandora's approval, Whistler and Lila climbed with Seabold down the rocky cliff to the shore.

Halfway down, Seabold could see the otter out in the water, hanging on to the fog buoy and rocking it back and forth with all his might. This made the buoy bell ring as loudly and clearly as if a mighty storm were tossing the water.

"Help!" called the otter. "Hurry!"

Seabold and the children hurried. They climbed into Seabold's boat and quickly arrived at the buoy.

"Oh, thank you for coming!" said the otter gratefully. "My name is Dooley, and my sister, Dottie, is in trouble."

"What kind of trouble?" asked Whistler and Lila at the same time.

Dooley explained that he and his sister had been playing tag on an abandoned boat anchored near Egg Island.

"And then," said the otter, his face looking quite serious, "Dottie got tangled in a sailor's net, and she can't get out."

"Oh dear," said Lila. And she and Whistler looked straight at Seabold to see what he might do.

Seabold had sailed so many oceans and had lived so many adventures that whatever a problem might be, if it involved the sea or a boat, he would have the solution. And for this problem, Seabold felt sure that he did.

"I know how to free your sister from that net," he said to Dooley.

"You do?" the otter asked hopefully.

"On which side of Egg Island is this boat?" asked Seabold.

"Southwest," answered Dooley.

"Swim back," Seabold instructed, "and we will be there very soon. Right now I have to find some dolphins."

"Dolphins?" asked Whistler. "What can dolphins do?"

They all looked at Seabold.

"Race," said Seabold with a smile. "Dolphins can race."

3. Dolphins!

Things began to happen very quickly once Seabold had a plan. Dooley the otter went swimming back to his sister, Seabold and the children returned to the lighthouse, and soon Pandora was speaking to one of the gulls who liked to rest on the sill outside the lantern room. The gull's name was Rufus.

"Can you find the dolphins quickly?" asked Pandora.

"I know exactly where the dolphins are," said Rufus, "because we had a race this morning."

"Will you fly to them and tell them we need them right away?" asked Pandora.

And before she could say thank you, Rufus was off.

In the kitchen Whistler and Lila were packing a lunch for Dooley and his entangled sister.

"They will probably be very thirsty," said Lila, pouring wild raspberry juice into a pitcher Seabold had carved from a gourd. She popped a large acorn nut into the spout.

"And hungry," said Whistler, wrapping the elderberry fritters left from breakfast into one of Pandora's tea towels.

Seabold watched out the window and soon saw Rufus signaling him to the shore.

"Let's go, children!" said Seabold. "Hurry!"

"Good luck!" called Pandora as she and Tiny waved good-bye to them.

When they reached the shore, Seabold and the children found twelve dolphins leaping out of the water and spinning and bobbing and talking excitedly among themselves.

"There they are!" said one of the dolphins.

They swam up to the rock where Seabold waited with Whistler and Lila.

"How can we help?" all twelve said at the same time, bobbing their noses up and down.

"We have to find a school of sawfish," said Seabold. "Can you guide us there?"

"Oh yes!" came twelve answers.

Then Seabold, Whistler, and Lila were soon sailing in *Adventure*, its little bow surrounded by twelve speeding, dazzling, acrobatic, exceptionally good-humored dolphins.

In their wake, the little boat sailed faster and farther than ever before.

And Whistler and Lila discovered they adored racing.

4. Egg Island

The dolphins soon found the sawfish, and the entire school said that most certainly they would be happy to help. So the dolphins went off to play, and Seabold, Whistler, and Lila sailed toward Egg Island with a very capable school of sawfish following close behind.

"I see them!" cried Lila when the abandoned boat appeared in the distance. "We brought juice!" she called.

"And fritters!" yelled Whistler.

In no time at all the sawfish were sawing vigorously at the rope trapping the young otter.

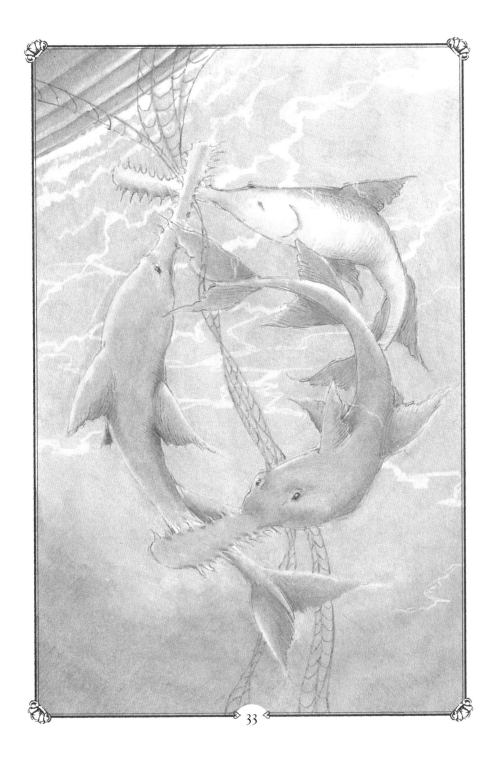

Lila tried to comfort Dottie as the sawfish worked. She told her stories about mermaids, which helped the mood all around.

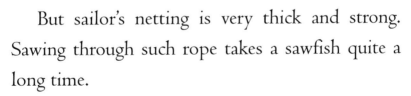

But sailor's netting is very thick and strong. Sawing through such rope takes a sawfish quite a long time.

And the sun was now setting. And soon the sea would be dark.

Poor Dottie, all tangled and trapped, became more and more afraid as the sun's light disappeared. She started to cry.

"Oh dear," said Whistler, Lila, Seabold, and Dooley all together. The sawfish might have said this too, had they not been so busy.

But just then, in the darkness, the water all around them began to glow. It glowed, brighter and brighter, and as it did, Dottie's tears stopped flowing.

"Jellyfish!" said Whistler.

Even the luminescent jellyfish had come to help.

So with everyone doing everything they possibly could to help young Dottie, finally she was set free.

She hugged her brother first, and then she hugged Seabold, Whistler, and Lila. She blew kisses to the fish.

And as the sawfish and the jellyfish swam away, everyone who was left behind ate elderberry fritters and drank warm raspberry juice in the lovely night.

5. Friends and Dumplings

One morning not long after this amazing nighttime rescue, Dooley and Dottie showed up at the cottage door of the lighthouse family. The otters looked quite happy, and everyone was glad to see them.

"We have come to do something for *you* now," explained Dottie. "To repay you for your bravery and your kindness."

"Oh no," said Whistler, "it was no bother at all. In fact, we quite enjoyed it."

"Nevertheless, here we are," said Dooley.

He then pulled a small hammer from his pocket. "I am very good with tools," he said.

Dottie pulled a pincushion from her pocket. "And I am very good with a needle," she said.

"What can we make for you?" they asked together.

So by day's end, Pandora had a beautiful new cedar barrel planted with radishes and carrots. And Lila and Tiny had five new dresses for their dolls.

Everyone ate a large bowl of yam dumplings, and then Dottie and Dooley left for home, holding hands as otters do.

It was so nice to have made new friends.